The Sleepover Club

Have you been invited to all these sleepovers?

Sleepover Club Makeover

by Jana Hunter

Collins

An imprint of HarperCollins*Publishers*

The Sleepover Club ® is a
Registered trademark of HarperCollins*Publishers* Ltd

First published in Great Britain by Collins in 2003
Collins is an imprint of HarperCollins*Publishers* Ltd
77-85 Fulham Palace Road, Hammersmith,
London W6 8JB

The HarperCollins website address is
www.**fire**and**water**.com

1 3 5 7 9 8 6 4 2

Text copyright © Jana Novotny Hunter 2003

Original series characters, plotlines
and settings © Rose Impey 1997

ISBN 0 00 711800 7

The author asserts the moral right to
be identified as the author of the work.

Printed and bound in England by
Clays Ltd, St Ives plc

Sleepover Kit List

1. Sleeping bag
2. Pillow
3. Pyjamas or a nightdress
4. Slippers
5. Toothbrush, toothpaste, soap etc
6. Towel
7. Teddy
8. A creepy story
9. Food for a midnight feast:
   chocolate, crisps, sweets, biscuits.
   In fact anything you like to eat.
10. Torch
11. Hairbrush
12. Hair things like a bobble or hairband,
    if you need them
13. Clean knickers and socks
14. Change of clothes for the next day
15. Sleepover diary and membership card

CHAPTER ONE

Hi, how are you doing? Have you come to see the play? I've saved you a front-row seat. Excuse me, I must get on. I've got a ton of little black noses to paint before curtain time…

We've got a conveyor belt going. Lots of little squirrels and weasels and bunnies, to say nothing of baby hedgehogs. Frankie is doing the spiky faces and Kenny is doing the furry ones. Rosie is doing the eyes and Lyndz is doing the whiskers. Our practice in Musical Make-up is a big help. (I'll tell you about Musical Makeovers, when I've got a second to spare. Right now this is a madhouse.)

The music starts and the beautiful, the wonderful, *new* school curtains swish open.

Phew! Maybe this is a good moment to tell you all about it. You know, why the Sleepover Club is helping with the make-up and costumes for the Cuddington Players' production of *The Wind in the Willows* and all that.

What? You don't know what the Sleepover Club is? Where have you been living, Planet Nowhere? No, sorry. I don't mean to be rude or anything, but everyone knows about the most coo-el gang of girls ever to hit Cuddington! We are: Frankie, Kenny, Lyndz, Rosie and me, Fliss (Felicity Proudlove in case you didn't know). Our gang is famous for its ace sleepovers where we have fun with a capital F. We're also famous for getting into trouble with a capital T, but it's not our fault. We just can't stop ourselves when we get going. Anyway, before all the big trouble with the clingfilm and the spots and the horror of being hauled off to prison for causing permanent damage to Molly the Monster's face, we have to go back to the beginning...

It all started a few weeks ago in Assembly. Mrs Poole, our headmistress, was making an announcement about the Cuddington Players.

"This year," she said, "the Cuddington Players will be using our very own school stage to put on their production of *The Wind in the Willows*. And I think they're going to want some of you little ones to be animals…"

There was the usual Cuddington Juniors' excitement as the infants bounced about and squealed. And in the hullabaloo, Lyndz leant over and hissed, "Yeah, and my dad's the producer of the play!"

Lindsey's dad, Keith, is Head of the Art Department at the Comprehensive we're going to after Year Six. But as if that wasn't enough, he produces plays with the Cuddington Players in his spare time!

"The only trouble is," Mrs Poole was going on, "we *still* don't have any curtains for our stage…"

Right on cue the whole school went, "*Ohhhh*…" just like the Teletubbies when they don't want to wave bye-bye.

Mrs Poole nodded. "Yes, *'Ohhhh'*. We can't have a play without curtains now, can we?"

"Noooo, Mrs Poole..." went all the little infants in the front row, as if they remembered last year's school play when everyone had to line up on stage for the final bow in complete darkness (so the audience wouldn't see us) and we all landed in one gigantic heap on the floor. You should've seen us, it was well funny. Ooops, sorry. I was telling you about Mrs Poole's announcement, wasn't I? Honestly, I am such a fluff-brain, sometimes...

"So what are we going to do about it, boys and girls?" Mrs Poole continued. "Any ideas? Hands up!"

There was silence while everyone thought hard. Then, suddenly, hands started going up all over the hall.

"Miss, we could paint pretend curtains!" said a little kid.

"Or borrow the curtains from the windows in the hall," suggested the gruesome Emily Berryman in her gruff goblin voice.

"Yes, Miss," simpered her goody-goody mate, Emma Hughes. "We could take them down and... blah blah blah..." (That girl loves the sound of her own voice.)

But luckily Mrs Poole said "no" to the totally stoo-pid hall curtain idea. If she hadn't, we'd never have heard the last of it from our sworn enemies the M&Ms (that's the Sleepover Club's nickname for the Gruesome Twosome, by the way).

The whole school went on suggesting things and some of the ideas were truly sad, like lining up the dustbins on stage, or having a row of kids to shield the performers, or even dear old Kenny's lame-brain idea of draping swimming towels over ladders! (I ask you!)

At this rate the Cuddington Players would have what you might call a naked stage.

Then, Frankie the Wizz had one of her brilliant ideas. "Miss, why don't we have a fundraiser to buy new curtains?"

We've had fundraisers before, and our gang are ace at them.

"That's an excellent idea, Francesca," beamed Mrs Poole and all the teachers nodded delightedly. "Don't you think so, boys and girls?"

The whole school went, "Yes, Mrs Poole!" while Lyndz and I thumped Frankie on the back to congratulate her.

"Three cheers for Frankie!" shouted out Kenny. "Hip, hip, *hooray*!"

Well, you know how a bunch of school kids can get totally mad sometimes? This was one of those times. The cheering and clapping started big time, and I mean big time. (One little kid got so excited he wet himself!) When that happened Mrs Poole frowned and told us to go to our classrooms and work on our fundraiser ideas *sensibly*.

So that's how our class competition came up. It was the cute, the completely dishy, Ryan Scott's idea. He's definitely the best-looking boy in our school and luckily he happens to be in my class! (My mum says I'm too young to go out with boys, but when I look at Ryan Scott I know she's dead wrong.)

Anyway, our teacher, Mrs Weaver, thought Ryan was the bee's knees too right then, because she thought his idea was just as brilliant as Frankie's. "Yes, Ryan," she gushed. "I think if we have a class competition to raise the most money, we'll have the curtains in no time!"

"In *Cuddington Playtime* you mean, Miss!" joked Kenny and everyone, including Mrs

Weaver, laughed. (Mrs Weaver might be strict sometimes, but you can always have a joke with her if you get her in the right mood.)

"YAY!" the whole class cheered.

A competition! Did I tell you Cuddington School was the best?

CHAPTER TWO

"I know what we could do!" Lyndz was mega excited at the thought of helping out her dad. "We could give pony rides!"

Lyndz is horse mad, and she's always trying to get as many rides in as she can.

But practical Rosie knocked that one on the head. "I'm scared of horses," she reminded Lyndz. "And anyway, what about the little kids?"

"They'd most likely wet the saddle," giggled Kenny, and we all burst out laughing, remembering the kid in Assembly.

So pony rides were O-U-T out.

We were trying to come up with fundraiser ideas for our team. Mrs Weaver had split the class into groups and told us to give each team a name. Ours was the *Sleepover Gang* (natch!) and the goody-goody M&M's were, can't you guess… the *Little Angels*. (Puke!) They were so jealous that Frankie had come up with the fundraiser idea, they were determined to show the world what little darlings they were (NOT!) and win.

"What about a sponsored bike ride?" suggested Rosie. But everyone said that was no good because Ryan Scott's team, *Hot Wheels*, was bound to do that.

"We could have a jumble sale," said Frankie. (Personally I think she had used up all her good ideas in one shot with the fundraiser scheme.) "You know, collect rubbish and sell it."

"Yeah, I could put my house in it," muttered Rosie to herself. Rosie's house was a bit of a tip since her dad, the builder, had left and sometimes it got her down.

"Or put the M&M's rubbish team up for sale…"

"Yeah."

"So what about a jumble sale, then?" persisted Frankie, and I could tell she had something up her sleeve. When the Wizz gets that "look" anything can happen!

"*Bor-ing*!" Kenny yawned. "A sponsored football match would be much more coo-el."

"Yeah, and who'd be on the team?" I wanted to know. "Not me, that's for sure."

Kenny pretended to do a header right in my face. "*Goal*!" she cheered and Mrs Weaver looked over to quieten us down.

"Well, what about an animal show, then?" (Lyndz could never let go of her favourite subject.) "I could borrow a horse from the stables and parade it on stage."

"Whoever heard of a horse on stage?" laughed Frankie, and she reared like a stallion, bashing into the book display and making it topple over.

"You've heard of a *stage* coach, haven't you?" Lyndz grinned.

"D'you want to go on the *stage*?" chuckled Rosie. "There's one leaving in two minutes!"

That started us off on one of our horsey

16

joke fests. The jokes were well daft. Read them and you'll see what I mean:

Q. Heard the one about the pantomime horse who tripped over his own tail?
A. He didn't know which end was up!

Q. How d'you hire a horse?
A. You put two bricks under him!

Book Titles:

Twenty Years in the Saddle by Major Bumsore
Desert Cactus Cowboy by Evan Sorer
Rodeo Rider by I. Hangon

We were killing ourselves so much by then it made Kenny do her horse whinny imitation and soon we were mucking about, in true sleepover style, snorting and neighing away. Any moment now, Lyndz would start hiccuping.

"Er, *Sleepover Gang*, if you can't do this sensibly…" began Mrs Weaver and the M&Ms smirked gleefully at the prospect of us getting into trouble.

"Sorry, Miss," said Frankie innocently. "We were only trying out ideas."

"Well, try them out *quietly*," warned Mrs Weaver. She was busy drawing up a huge graph (probably planning on a major Maths project) and she looked like she meant business.

"Yes, Mrs Weaver."

We seriously got back down to it, then. This was a better skive than slogging away in our Maths workbooks, and we didn't want to ruin the chance for a laugh. So for a while the Sleepover Gang acted more angelic than the goody-goody M&Ms themselves.

Mind you, all the time the rest of the gang were talking and thinking I was fizzing away inside, like a firework ready to explode. See, I had this brilliant idea. The coolest, most wonderful brainwave I'd ever had in my entire life. Oh, you're wondering why I didn't come right out with it, are you? Well, it's weird. When something matters to me, you know like, *really* matters, I can sometimes go all shy about it, even round my best friends. D'you ever get like that?

Suddenly, though, I couldn't hold it in any longer. "Let's have a *Makeover*!" I blurted out, and I could tell my cheeks had gone bright red with excitement. "You know, make up people and charge for it."

"Coo-el!" said Lyndz

"We could even give fashion advice and dress people up..." I was getting really excited.

Rosie interrupted me. "Where would we get the class gear for that?"

"We could borrow glamorous gear from my gran's dress shop. And make stuff out of our own clothes..." I began, but football-mad Kenny couldn't let that one go.

"*Glamorous* gear. How girlie-girlie!" Kenny (who lives in her Leicester City football strip) wrinkled her nose in disgust.

I could feel myself going red, and bit my lip.

"Using your own clothes is all right for you," Frankie laughed, giving my long blonde hair a playful tug. "A Fashion Victim like you has got the best gear in the whole school."

I blushed even harder. Can I help it if I love clothes and make-up? It's a Proudlove family tradition.

"We could use my mum's dressing-up clothes," offered Lyndz, whose mum has the best dressing-up box ever.

I flashed Lyndz a grateful smile. (She's the soft-hearted one in our gang and you can always rely on her to rescue you.)

"Anyway, we don't need flash gear," I explained, feeling a bit more confident. "We can use old stuff and make it totally fab."

"How?" asked Rosie suspiciously.

"You know, decorate T-shirts and jeans with sequins and beads and stuff! We could do fabric paint designs, embroider flowers and sew on floaty bits…" I'm going to be a fashion designer when I grow up and I couldn't wait to try out some of my own gorgeous designs.

"Hmmm…" mused Frankie and I could see she was getting into it. Frankie is also known as Spaceman because she loves jewellery, sequins and nail varnish – anything as long as it's silver.

"We could sell jewellery," I prompted her, dead innocent like.

"Yeah! We could make our own!" said Frankie excitedly. "I was thinking of selling some of mine at the jumble sale anyway."

So that was it. Frankie was never one to let go a chance to thread beads and glue diamonds. That's why she'd been so keen to have a boring old jumble sale.

I wasn't complaining, though, 'cos Frankie's vote tipped the balance. And suddenly the gang saw that a Makeover was the neatest, sweetest little plan that yours truly had ever come up with!

Of course, Kenny had to be the fly in the ointment. "Oh, no, a Makeover!" she groaned, making out to stick her fingers down her throat. "Urrrgh!"

"It'll be fun," I retorted. "We can get ideas for outfits to wear to my Auntie Jill's wedding."

"The wedding, of course!" Lyndz squealed excitedly.

"Hey, that'd be great," Frankie agreed.

My Auntie Jill, our very own Snowy Owl from Brownies, is a big favourite with our gang (especially now she's marrying Mark, our old tennis instructor). And Auntie Jill had promised that her wedding would be "different" (which could mean anything with

21

my crazy auntie) so I reckoned a Makeover was a golden opportunity to make fab gear for it. Trouble is, I'd forgotten how Kenny *hates* weddings and romance almost as much as she hates frilly clothes, girlie-girlie colours and make-up.

"Pass me the vomit bag!" she heaved.

I could see Kenny was going to take a lot of convincing, but funnily enough it was the ghastly M&Ms (earwigging as usual) who changed her mind.

"You lot doing Makeovers!" they sneered. "What do you know? You're too *ugly!*"

"You lot as Little Angels!" I snapped right back. "You're too *nasty!*"

"Just wait till we do all our good turns," sniffed Emma huffily.

"We'll have the whole of Cuddington eating out of our hands," agreed the Goblin in her horrible gruff voice.

"Yeah, yeah, *yeah*…"

They went on winding us up about how they were going to win the prize, by running errands and doing odd jobs. Totally sick-making. Mind you, we gave back as good as we got. We pointed out that scrubbing floors and babysitting bratty kids wasn't half so much fun as doing makeovers, and they knew it.

Huh! One-nil to the Sleepover Gang! But before Total War could break out, Mrs Weaver was clapping her hands for everyone to be quiet.

"Year Six, I've made this graph," she announced, holding up a huge sheet of coloured card, "to show the progress of your fundraising competition. (So the graph wasn't for Maths! Phew!) "It has the name of every team in the class, and Mrs Poole informs me that the Cuddington Players will award a prize to the winning team."

A prize for the winning team!

The Sleepover Gang *had* to get it.

There was only one thing to do. Have a Sleepover to work on our make-up skills. Luckily, we were having one at my house that night!

Look out, *Little Angels*!

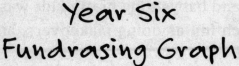

Year Six
Fundrasing Graph

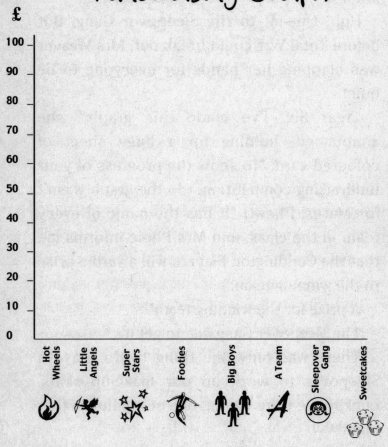

CHAPTER THREE

If my mum could have seen the state of our living room she'd have had a blue fit. I'd tipped my make-up drawer on to the sofa and there was lip gloss, nail varnish, body glitter, transfers and tiny pots of eye gel strewn all over it. It was even spilling on to Mum's prized white carpet.

Well, it was her fault for making us have our Sleepover in the living room. (Since the last Sleepover we've had to use the living room so we wouldn't wake up the twins. Cheek!)

So we were trying to make the best of it. Frankie was threading beads and Lyndz was stretched out on the floor, surrounded by all her art stuff. (She was working on the poster advertising our Makeover.)

"What about this?" she said, holding up a drawing of a girl covered in make-up.

"Aaagh! The curse of the *pink lippy*!" Kenny screamed, and before I could rescue my make-up, she'd done a pretend faint backwards right on to it.

"*Kenny*!" I tried to rescue my multi-coloured eye shimmer palette from under Kenny's bum.

Kenny lifted one thigh unhelpfully. "Ooops." Then, seeing I wasn't laughing, she got all businesslike to prove she wasn't just being a nuisance. (Huh!)

"I think it's time we made some group decisions," she said pointedly, flipping open her Sleepover diary. "So. Who's doing what?"

Er, actually this was all my idea, but I let Kenny get on with running the show. You know Kenny. Bossing everyone around would get her into the mood for makeovers, pink lippy or no pink lippy.

"Jewellery by Frankie!" announced Frankie, looking up from the tray of beads balanced on her knees.

Kenny wrote that down. Then Frankie piped up again, "Oh, and I'll do face painting."

"Wh – what do you mean?" I spluttered. "You're doing the jewellery."

Frankie threw me a withering look. "And who has the face paints?"

My cheeks burned. "But I want to do make-up..." I finished lamely.

Kenny closed her eyes and sighed. "So, if you do regular make-up, Frankie can do face painting. OK?"

I busied myself with putting the top back on a lip gloss.

"*Well?*"

There was a silence, where it felt like everyone was thinking what a selfish thing I was to demand my rights. But it wasn't like that. This was the first time in ages I'd had a major idea and Kenny was acting like it was nothing. I was shoved out at home and now I was shoved out with my best friends. It wasn't fair.

Then good old Rosie chimed in, changing the subject. "I'll do style makeovers in school and charge for them," she said. (Her favourite TV show's where they take someone with really awful dress sense and change her image completely. Now Rosie-posie wanted to do the same on some fashion disaster.)

"OK, 'Rosie – style makeovers'." Kenny wrote it down in her Sleepover diary. "So who's doing hair?"

Pointing our fingers at her, we all shouted out, "*YOU*!"

"Noooo!" groaned Kenny, but you could tell she was secretly pleased. Her mum does hairdressing at home so she must have learnt something. Actually, hair was one of the other things I was dying to do, but there was no way I could make a fuss now, was there?

Lyndz consoled Kenny as if doing hair was a punishment. "You can practise haircutting on us, Kenny."

(Not on my hair, she won't! I vowed.)

"You'll all probably end up bald!" Kenny warned, but she wrote down her speciality just the same.

I was feeling well bad that everyone had latched on to Kenny's ideas so quickly. Didn't my ideas count for anything? But it meant so much for the *Sleepover Gang* to beat the *Little*

Angels in the competition, so I had to give in! And I have to admit it was fun getting into it. In the end, this is what we came up with:

1. Fliss – beauty treatments and make-up
2. Rosie – style makeovers
3. Lyndz – advertising and manicures
4. Frankie – jewellery and face painting
5. Kenny – hairdressing

"We should do a 'Swap the Head' challenge," giggled Lyndz, when it was all written down in Kenny's diary.

"What's that?"

"You know, you cut up pictures of people and swap their heads around. Then you charge for guessing whose body belongs where."

Frankie gave a snort of laughter. "I can just see Emily Berryman's body with the school hamster's head!"

"And Mrs Pickernose with its bum!"

"*Wicked*!"

Mrs Pickernose is our name for our gruesome dinner lady, Mrs Pickett. (Mind you, Pickett is a good name for her too, because she's always picking on us lot.)

"Imagine Dishy Dave with Mr Short's knobbly knees!" laughed Rosie.

We'd seen Mr Short's knees when he wore shorts at the school fête and they were well knobbly.

"Oh, Dave, Dave!" I sighed, pretending to swoon. "I never *knew* your knees were so knobbly!"

Everyone shrieked with laughter and Lyndz went into a major bout of hiccups (natch!). We had to bash her on the back, and scare her with horrible faces, to try and stop her.

Suddenly, there was a loud banging on the ceiling that made us all jump out of our skins. "Keep it down in there!" my mum called out. "I'm trying to get the twins to bed."

As if we didn't know. Already, the babies' ear-splitting howls were interrupting our important Sleepover Gang business. Why couldn't *they* be the ones to "keep it down", I'd like to know? Those twins were taking over the whole house!

And as if that wasn't bad enough, Mum's knocking had made the gang go embarrassingly quiet. I knew just what they were thinking…

My mum used to do all sorts of cool things for our sleepovers, making scrummy things to eat and treating us dead grown-up, but these days all she could think of was my baby brother and sister. Sleepovers were nothing but a nuisance to her since they came along and now she'd banished us to the living room it was even worse. It was really winding me up.

Didn't I count for anything in this house any more?

"I know," I said, trying to shrug it off, "let's play Musical Make-up." (Those twins were not going to ruin *my* Sleepover!)

"Musical Make-up. *Brillo*!" squealed Frankie, forgetting to be quiet. She leapt up, knocking her tray of beads all over the floor.

Who cares? I thought. We'll clean up later.

Musical Make-up is the Sleepover Gang's own version of musical chairs. Difference is, when the music stops, instead of just finding a chair, you plonk yourself opposite someone. Then the two of you make up one side of the other's face (*both working at the same time!*). You have to work dead fast before the music starts up again, and the winner is the person with the finished face. You get some really weird faces, half one way and half another.

"OK," I said, turning up the music recklessly. "Line up the chairs."

There was lots of giggling as we squashed four dining-room chairs between the two sofas. "Now. Ready, steady, GO!"

There wasn't room to move, so my friends kept banging into things and falling over one another. They got well daft. But when I stopped the music they went totally haywire. Rosie and Lyndz got going on each other, while Frankie and Kenny partnered up. They worked fast and furious, making up one side of each other's face.

"I can't see to do your lips!" screeched Rosie, as Lyndz plastered eye gel over her closed eyelid. Rosie blindly tried to do Lyndz's lips, but the lip gloss went all over her chin.

"You've got a pink beard!" shrieked Frankie.

Lyndz groaned. "Oh, noooo."

"Look at Kenny!" chortled Frankie as she finished pencilling in one surprised eyebrow.

Before she had a chance to do any more, I turned the music back on. The four of them shrieked, and looking like clowns with split personalities, they leapt up for the second round.

"ONE STEP CLOSER TO HEAVEN, BABEEEEE!" pounded the music and we all joined in, singing loud and proud.

Suddenly, the living-room door flew open and my mum burst in, clutching a furiously squalling baby on either arm. "Turn that down, this minute!" she demanded. (I suppose she had to shout, what with the music and the twins screaming their heads off, but she didn't need to sound so cross.)

I punched the control button and everyone (except the twins) froze.

My mum glared at me over one squalling baby head. "This is the last Sleepover in this house, Felicity Proudlove," she informed me angrily. "The absolute last."

"But, Mum…"

"And as for the rest of you, I shall speak to your parents in the morning!"

"Mum, you can't…" I burst into tears. "*You just can't!*"

"Waaa! Waaa! Waaa!" (Yes, she can! Yes, she can!) yelled the stoopid twins in unison.

CHAPTER FOUR

Back at school, things only got worse. (It was that stupid graph's fault. It told the whole class the terrible truth.)

The *Sleepover Gang* was losing to *Hot Wheels*.

"Can't beat speed!" Ryan Scott teased, and just catching his eye made my cheeks go pink. "*Hot Wheels* rule!" he grinned.

"*Don't*!" I begged, dropping my bag of lip gloss, blushers and glitter gels all over the classroom floor.

"Don't what?" Ryan asked, dead innocent.

"Er… Ryan, let me put it this way…" Frankie

34

began, as she helped retrieve the jars rolling about the floor. "*Shut up!*"

Ryan looked at me and grinned his gorgeous grin, but the dreaded Emma Hughes had to go and spoil my wonderful moment (natch!). "Don't know why you bother," she sneered. "The *Little Angels* will beat you both!" And she flounced out the classroom as if she'd already won.

That girl is a sad case.

Mind you, the *Sleepover Gang* had to work fast to beat the opposition, so it was dead lucky we had a super coo-el plan...

Welcome to the Cuddington Juniors MAKEOVER with me on make-up, Kenny on hair, Rosie on fashion, Frankie on jewellery and Lyndz on manicures.

Yep, this break time the *Sleepover Gang* was ready to beautify anyone who wanted to be beautiful. I'd brought enough make-up to do the whole school and with a team like us, we could even make Mrs Pickernose look good. (Well, not exactly good, but you know what I mean.) Beauty has its price, of course, and ours was £1 a go. (Mind you, seeing how much the *Hot Wheels* had already made, maybe a price increase was on the cards!)

"See you, *losers*!" teased Ryan, revving up his imaginary hot wheels, right into me.

"*Ry-YAN*!" I squealed, as he screeched by me and zoomed off into the playground. Who needs blusher when Ryan Scott's around?

Outside in the playground, girls swarmed around us like bees to a honey pot.

"Do me first!"

"No, me."

"*Me*," went Alana Palmer, who was so keen to look good she forgot whose side she was on.

"Me!" begged Gemma Hitchins.

We had them lining up!

Only trouble was, some of our clients hadn't brought any money, so in the end we let them pay with sweets or packets of crisps.

"The idea is to sell those sweets at lunch time, not eat them!" I protested as Lyndz stuffed her face with a Penguin bar.

"Just this one," Lyndz pleaded, through a mouthful of chocolate crumbs. "I'm starved!"

"Me too," groaned Kenny. "Give us that Curly Whirly."

"I'll have a KitKat," said Frankie.

"And me," piped up Rosie.

Our profits were disappearing fast. One of us had to make some money round here, and it looked like it had to be me.

"Right," I said, laying out tubes of gel and pots of face glitter on my pink Barbie towel. "Gemma Hitchins, I'll do you first."

Gemma squealed with delight and perched on the special Makeover stool (actually the playground's concrete turtle we all used to climb on in Year One).

I gave a professional cough, like my mum, the beautician, always did with awkward clients. "Ahem. Now, let's start with skin care..." You'd think making up girls would be easy, but Gemma Hitchins was a challenge because she wanted all her freckles to disappear! (And Gemma Hitchins had more freckles than a greater spotted toad with measles.)

"I'm a make-up artist, not a magician," I sighed. "Can't you go for a country girl look?"

"No," said Gemma shaking her ginger head. "Get rid of them!" But even three layers of my mum's thick cover stick couldn't do that. Those orange blobs kept popping back up like some dreaded lurgy! The only way was to concentrate on Gemma's green eyes (sort of to distract you from the freckles). So I applied masses of green glitter eye gel, while next to me, Kenny got going on Alana Palmer's (otherwise known as drippy Alana Banana's) hair.

"What does Madam want today?" Kenny said, picking out a bit of Curly Whirly from her teeth. "How about French plaits?"

Alana Banana shook her head. "Cut it!" she ordered, freeing a huge bunch of frizzy hair from its scrunchie.

"Oooh... kay," Kenny said doubtfully. "If you're sure that's what you want."

The dopey girl nodded from under her big bush of hair. "I want to look like a famous model."

Kenny and I exchanged "looks" over Alana Banana's head.

Kenny got out her scissors and started hacking away. And from the way she worked, you could tell it was not the same as cutting straight hair, 'cos you couldn't see if you were

38

getting it even with all that frizz. And no matter how much water or hair wax Kenny slicked on, Alana's hair still sprung out from her head like an electric Brillo pad.

"It's got a mind of its own!" moaned Kenny, hopelessly trying to hold it down with a comb.

Alana Banana groaned. "I know. That's why my mum makes me wear it long and pulled back."

Shorter and shorter Kenny chopped, but the effect was more and more like Basil Brush on a bad day. "Maybe if I give you a skinhead at the sides it'll look better," Kenny sighed. "It can't look any worse."

Oh, couldn't it? Snip, snip, snip. Alana's buzzed-out hairdo gave new meaning to the phrase "bad hair day".

"You've made me look like a clown!" shrieked Alana when Kenny finally admitted defeat and handed her the mirror.

"You could always wear a wig."

"My mum's gonna kill me…"

But there was no time for Kenny to worry about Alana Banana's mum. Four girls were already lining up for spray-in hair colour while another hopeful wanted a fringe.

It made the job of improving my next customer, a goofy girl, seem easy. "Smile," I ordered as I slicked lashings of *Lip Fizzlin' Lip Tint* on to her mouth, and the girl obeyed with a dazzling grin. Trouble was, when she smiled her teeth were so big I got blackcurrant gel all over them.

Danny McCloud, who was watching the whole operation with Ryan, laughed his silly head off. "I've seen better teeth on a comb!" he sniggered as I wiped my client's teeth with a tissue.

"Shut up!" I growled at him.

"Yeth, thut up!" lisped the goofy girl.

"Take no notice," I said to her. "You look lovely."

And the truth was, she did.

"Do me next," Ryan said as Kenny finished her client's fringe. "I want an orange mohawk."

"Get lost."

I knew what Danny and Ryan were up to. They wanted to put us off so *Hot Wheels* would keep on winning. So, on a silent signal, we just blanked them out. (Not easy when one of them is so dishy his eyes burn holes in your back.)

But ignore them or not, the tension was still rising, and Lyndz was having a terrible time slopping blobs of nail varnish everywhere but her client's nails. It was like the curse of the blobs. But it was when Rosie was giving advice on colour that real disaster struck.

"Green is definitely your colour," Rosie was saying sweetly to a girl in Year Five, Mandy Owen.

"Yeah, matches the bogeys up your nose!" snickered Danny.

Rosie gritted her teeth and ploughed on. "You know, you'd look great in really tight hipsters..."

"Yeah, her bum would look like two boiled eggs in a handkerchief!" persisted Danny.

Rosie ignored him, but Mandy flushed an angry red colour.

"In fact," Rosie finished desperately, "you'd look good in anything!"

"Yeah, anything except a mirror!" and Danny and Ryan broke up laughing. "You..."

41

But before Danny could say another word, Mandy had leapt up, grabbed Lyndz's manicure tray and bashed him over the head with it.

"OW!"

Bottles of ruby, blue and purple nail varnish slid down Danny's face and shattered on to the playground in millions of sticky pools of colour. They ran across the tarmac in a rainbow swirl.

"My nail varnish!" screamed Lyndz. "I'll get you for this, Danny McCloud!"

"Try it!" dared Danny, and he and Ryan legged it across the playground with Lyndz haring after them screaming for blood.

CHAPTER FIVE

Some hope! The only blood spilt was mine when I cut myself on a broken nail varnish bottle. (Mrs Weaver was not best pleased.)

"What have you been up to?" she demanded, dabbing my finger with stingy antiseptic.

"Ouch! Er… it was an accident," I began but Emma Hughes, 'The Queen', couldn't resist the chance to get us in trouble.

"Miss, the *Sleepover Gang* were putting make-up and stuff on *everyone*!" went the squealer.

"*And* cutting hair!" barked the Goblin.

Those two are right telltales. And didn't they

just love it when Mrs Weaver called the gang up to her desk for what she calls "a little talking to"!

"But, Miss, we were only trying to raise money," protested Frankie. "Mrs Poole said we should use our initiative."

"That's all very well, Francesca," said Mrs Weaver severely, "but you should've got permission first."

"Yes, Miss."

"You could have caused a real accident bringing scissors into school," she went on, as if we were babies.

Blah, blah, blah…

It was well humiliating. And it wasn't helped by Alana Banana who kept clutching tufts of her cropped hair and wailing, "My mum's gonna go mad!"

The M&Ms were in fits of gleeful giggles at that. And for the rest of the afternoon, whenever Mrs Weaver noticed another girl with purple spiked hair, nail transfers or body glitter, her look of horror set them off again. They were in heaven. (Which I suppose is the best place for *Little Angels*, though, personally, I could think of a much *hotter* place.)

Anyway, their sniggering backfired this time because by the end of the afternoon the whole class, even the *Sleepover Gang*, was laughing. See, Mrs Weaver kept on going, "Oh no!" and "Shock, horror!" as she discovered another amazing hairdo or manicure. It was hilarious. Mrs Weaver was really playing up to it in the end, acting mega alarmed as she went round the class – even checking the boys' fingernails for polish and their eyelashes for mascara. And when Ryan fluttered his eyelashes like a girl, she even broke out laughing herself.

"Thank you, Ryan! You should audition for a part in the play," she chuckled as he preened and posed.

"Ohhh, thank you, thank you, Miss," Ryan gushed like a Hollywood film starlet.

It was well funny.

Of course, the M&M's laughter wasn't friendly. They couldn't bear everyone laughing *with* us and their sarcastic smirks were enough to make you sick.

Next day we wiped the smiles off their faces, though, when the *Sleepover Gang* overtook the *Hot Wheels* on the graph.

"YES!" Frankie and Kenny punched the air, while Lyndz, Rosie and I hugged each other. The *Sleepover Gang* was winning!

It was ace. We danced about and cheered like mad.

Too bad it didn't last. Because when the *Sweetcakes* gave in the money they'd collected from their bake sales, our victory bubble burst. The *Sweetcakes* were beating everyone!

Urrgh!

"Very good," beamed Mrs Weaver, when all the money was in. "Year Six, you are all doing really well."

"I wonder if the *Sweetcakes* baked *all* their own cakes," Emma Hughes hissed, accidentally-on-purpose getting Mrs Weaver to overhear.

"Or did their mums help them...?" finished the Goblin right on cue.

But Mrs Weaver, like the *Sleepover Gang*, had had it with the M&M's accusations. "That's enough, girls," she warned. "Be good sports, now." And both *Little Angels* flushed red as the fires of you-know-where!

Served them right.

In Maths that day, we did percentages and the *Sweetcakes* were beating us by 2%. They were also beating *Hot Wheels* by 4%. But the *Sleepover Gang* was beating the *Hot Wheels* by 1% and the *Little Angels* by 17%. No wonder the M&Ms had resorted to telling tales to wind us up. They were 100% losers!

It made Maths a really interesting subject, for a change. Especially since the graph was now a regular part of our Maths lesson. Every day it showed the different coloured teams moving up and up. Our class was making loads of money and the curtains looked more and more of a reality. Yep, everyone agreed school these days was more exciting than *Big Brother*.

Of course, the *Little Angels* were determined to beat us, each day edging up a little farther on the graph, so that by Thursday we were neck and neck. (Aaargh!) Those goody-goodies had been doing their sweet little 'helping out' stuff: running errands, walking dogs and babysitting, and they were cashing it in. (They even tried it in school, but most of the teachers refused to pay them for collecting books and handing in the registers. Good.) The best part was when the little darlings complained that it wasn't fair we'd got paid for advising teachers on fashion and hair, and nobody listened.

Two-nil to the *Sleepover Gang*!

Mind you, the *Little Angels* weren't the only ones getting their knickers in a twist. Oh no. The *Sweetcakes* fell out with their friends the *Super Stars* and the *A-Team* turned nasty with the *Footies*. When the *Hot Wheels* got into a fight with the *Big Boys* Mrs Weaver was not happy. She gave the whole class a huge talking to about "Healthy Competition and Rivalry" and said if there was any more unsporting behaviour, the whole thing would be cancelled.

That shut everyone up.

But the tension was rising as fast as the colours on the graph, and by Friday we all needed a break from it. Good thing it was a Sleepover night. What would we do without our fave, brilliant Sleepovers? Not be the *Sleepover Gang*, you say? Wash your mouth out with soap!

CHAPTER SIX

Tonight our Sleepover was at Rosie's, for a big change. (Rosie usually wheedles out of having Sleepovers at hers because, no matter how much we tell her it doesn't matter, she's still embarrassed about the state of her house.) But Rosie wanted to do a style makeover on her mum, so she relented.

"My mum dresses way too young," she confided as she opened the front door and let us in. "It's well embarrassing."

Rosie's mum, Karen, had gone back to college to qualify as a nursery nurse, and Rosie reckoned she dressed like the other students so as to keep up with them. Sometimes, Rosie said, she even borrowed her sister Tiffany's teenage gear!

I'd be so humiliated if my mum did that.

"Well, my mum's been wearing flowery skirts for years," said Kenny disgustedly, dumping her Sleepover kit in the hall. "She never wears trousers!"

"My mum's worn the same suits all her life," said Frankie, whose mum's a lawyer.

"Only difference now is they smell of baby sick!" I teased, stacking my sleeping bag neatly next to Frankie's.

Frankie groaned. "I know. And our car smells of nappies! Izzy always manages to fill hers the minute we get in!"

"Yuck!"

"I'd rather have dog poo any day," said Rosie. "Wouldn't I, Jenny?"

Jenny, Rosie's mongrel, sat up and panted as if to say "yes" and we all laughed.

"Your hall looks nice," Lyndz said, admiring the freshly painted walls and shampooed carpets.

"My mum's boyfriend did it," said Rosie.

"I love lilac," I said.

"Mmm. Wish Richard would hurry up and do the living room too."

"I like your living room the way it is," said Frankie, going in and throwing herself on to the big sagging couch.

"Yeah," agreed Kenny, kicking an imaginary football over to Frankie. "It's Chill Out City in here."

It was true. At Rosie's house you could really relax because her mum never worries about messes and stuff. Not like my mum.

I couldn't stop thinking about my mum since her go at me last Sleepover. See, me and my mum always used to talk about everything... Sleepovers, school, clothes, the house... But nowadays she never had time to have a natter over a plate of home-made cookies. It felt like she'd forgotten me.

And it was all the twins' fault.

"You're lucky you don't have baby brothers or sisters," I remarked to Rosie, studying the row of family photographs on the bookcase.

"No, I've got Adam," laughed Rosie just as Adam came bursting through the door in his electric wheelchair. Adam has cerebral palsy so he can't go anywhere without his "Mean Machine" (as he calls it).

"*Adam!*" Lyndz rushed over to get her usual ride on the back of the wheelchair.

"Hi."

"Wheee!" yelled Lyndz as the two of them zoomed about the room like loonies.

"Yee hee!" Adam laughed and his voice box screeched loudly.

Adam loves mucking about with us. You'd never believe how much you can understand him, even though he can't talk properly. His voice box and his expressions can tell you loads.

We each had a turn riding on the back of the Mean Machine and then Frankie got out her Sleepover kit. Tonight, she'd brought her face paints with her because she wanted to try out some designs to do on the little kids. "Cuddington's full of the little monsters," she said. "We can't afford to lose them as customers."

"You said it." I have to admit, even if Frankie does take over, she's good at making money.

52

Naturally, Adam wanted to get his face painted so Frankie agreed to try out her skills on him.

"Do one like the robot face you had at Animal World Wildlife Park," I said. "Remember when Lyndz was a tiger and I was a flower?"

"And Rosie was a frog?" said Kenny, who'd had her face painted in Leicester City colours. "That was well cool."

We all agreed that was great. So Frankie got to work. And while she turned Adam into a robot, Kenny gave him a haircut with her mum's electric clippers. Meanwhile, Lyndz spread out on the floor to work on a Swap the Head collage. (She planned to charge 25p a go for it.)

As for Rosie and me, we had more important things to do. *We had to turn Karen Cartwright into Rosie's dream mum!*

Upstairs, we started going through Rosie's mum's wardrobe. "We need to weed out the dross," said Rosie. "There's masses here." Luckily, Karen was working late at college and couldn't see what we were up to. As for Tiffany – she was too busy talking on the phone to even notice us. "This can go!" said Rosie, "And this, and this…" She was pulling things from their hangers and flinging them on to the floor.

"Are you sure your mum won't mind?" I said nervously, picking up the things Rosie was throwing out, so I could fold them into a neat pile. (I'm a total neatness freak, in case you didn't know.)

Rosie just shrugged. "Mum said she wanted a major chuck-out, so I'm helping her. Anyway, she can always get new stuff." Rosie knew as well as I did that her mum didn't have much money, but she was in an unusually reckless mood.

Suddenly, I had a brainwave. (Yes, Fliss the fluff-brain does have them sometimes, you know! Who was it thought of the Makeover, anyway?)

"Hey, my mum's put on a bit of weight since the twins were born and lots of her things don't fit her any more," I said. "Maybe they'll fit your mum."

"Fliss, you're the best!" Rosie jumped up and down on the bed. "Your mum's gear is coo-el."

It's true. My mum's fashion sense is top, like mine. (I've inherited my dress sense from her.) I reckoned Karen would look bang up-to-the-minute in some of my mum's things.

Two phone calls later, and it was all settled. My mum was trying to make it up to me for ruining our last Sleepover, so she was being as sweet as pie. She promised she would go through her wardrobe and see what Karen might like, and she'd bring it over when she got a chance.

Watch out Karen Cartwright! You're in for a style change bigger than any you've ever seen on telly!

Some Sleepovers are great and some are mega. Tonight's just started great and kept getting better. Everyone was in a party mood, so we decided to create some atmosphere. First we turned the lights down low and the music up loud. Then we piled cushions on to the floor to laze around on and spread out our Sleepover midnight feast – Cheesy Wotsits, crisps, M&Ms (the sweet kind!) and nuts – about the room in bowls.

"Let's *party*!" yelled Kenny, punching the air,

and we all danced about, singing loudly. Even Adam jerked his wheelchair in time to the music. He was well good too.

"You look like something out of *Star Wars*," giggled Lyndz, pointing to Adam's silver painted face.

Adam made robot noises and we all laughed.

"Paint my face too!" begged Rosie, slurping Coke down her chin.

"Mine too!" squealed Lyndz.

"And mine," I said.

So Frankie did all of us. She did Lyndz as a kitten, Rosie as a gypsy and me as Barbie (which according to her didn't take much). Even Kenny allowed her face to be painted in the red white and blue of the Union Jack! We looked ace.

Frankie, of course, did herself too. She was a lion with a furry face and black nose.

"Let's get *down*!" shouted Rosie and she put on *I'm the Urban Spaceman* loud and proud. We danced around the house, pulling Adam with us in circles, a spaceman, a kitten, a gypsy, a doll, a lion and a Union Jack.

"I'm the Urban Spaceman, Baby! I'm the one... I'M A LOTTA FUN!"

Man, the place rocked!

"Yeeeheee!" Adam was screeching away, being a robot.

Nobody heard Karen come in, and for a second she just stood there in shock, looking from one painted face to another. Then she cried very loud, over the music, "What happened to my little boy!"

"Bleep! Bleeep!" went Adam, screeching to a halt in front of her. "I. AM. A. ROBOT."

We all laughed. (All except Karen, that is.) Slowly, very slowly, she leaned forward and stroked Adam's shaved head. "A robot, eh?" she muttered. "Well, I liked you better as my little boy..."

"Bleep! Bleep!"

Karen had to laugh at that. She didn't like Adam's shaved head, but you could tell she was dead chuffed to see her "little boy" having so much fun.

"I must take a photo," she said, going to the stairs. "I'll get my camera..."

"WAIT! Mum, wait!" screamed Rosie, and she

57

hared up behind her mum in a desperate effort to get upstairs before her.

Too late.

"We are in the middle of…" began Rosie, but she was interrupted by a loud shriek of horror.

"*Aaargh!* I've been robbed!"

"HUH?" We all looked at each other.

"Robbed! My clothes, my wardrobe…"

"No, no it was us," interrupted Rosie, looking at her mum with a sickly sweet smile. "We just helped sort out your clothes for you."

"WHAT! You've stripped my wardrobe bare!" Karen was staring in shock at the one dress left hanging there.

"Not exactly bare…" Rosie protested feebly.

"*What do you think you were playing at?*"

But Rosie didn't have to answer. Because luckily, *very luckily*, this was the very moment my mum decided to arrive, carting three bulging carrier bags with her. (And, believe me, I've never been so pleased to see my mum in my entire life.)

"*Mum!*"

Mum smiled. "Tiffany said I could come up, Karen. I hope you don't mind."

Karen flopped back on to her bed, shaking her head in disbelief. "No, no. It's a relief to see another grown-up!" she sighed.

"I know just what you mean," smiled Mum.

"Just *look* at what these girls have been up to!"

"Oh dear," said Mum gravely, surveying the pile of discarded clothes. "The usual Sleepover Club madness, I see..."

"Yes..." agreed Karen, then suddenly her eyes met my mum's and they both burst out laughing.

"*The Sleepover Club madness*!" They went on and on saying it as if they'd discovered the joke of the century.

"Sometimes I feel like I'm living in a mad house!" said Karen hysterically.

"Me too! I had to get out of mine," shrieked my mum, "before I turned into a zombie..."

"So you thought you'd let Andy become one instead..."

"Yes. Let him babysit the twins for a ch-change..." They were both killing themselves by then, clutching their stomachs and wiping their eyes as if it was hilarious.

Rosie raised her eyebrows at me and all I could do was shrug.

Grown-ups! Can you figure them out?

CHAPTER SEVEN

We stayed up all night telling jokes and gorging on sweets. It was class. There was a huge moon shining right through Rosie's bedroom window and it felt like we were the only people on some silent planet.

We kept going over the evening and laughing at how daft the mums had been. You should've seen them. They were so giggly they'd opened a bottle of wine and both got well out of order. They'd screamed with laughter when the gang and I mucked about dancing and Karen insisted on taking photos of our painted faces. Then the two of them had a fashion fest – trying on each other's clothes, pretending to be in a teen video or something. Karen put on a pair of my mum's shorts and bikini top and danced about the bedroom like she was at a beach party while my mum played imaginary bongo drums and sang some old Elvis song.

It's embarrassing when grown-ups get silly like that. We're supposed to be the ones who do nutty stuff.

"Honestly, my mum's having her second childhood," I said, chomping on a Crunchie Bar in the silvery moonlight.

"And mine," agreed Rosie, plumping up her pillow. "I've even had to give her boyfriend advice!"

"And make her do her homework," chuckled Frankie.

"Exactly," said Rosie primly.

We all laughed at that. Since Karen was back to studying it was like she was the daughter and Rosie the grown-up.

"It reminds me of that joke," giggled Frankie.

Son: Mummy Mummy, I don't want to go to school.

62

Mother: Son, you have to go to school.

Son: But, Mummy, none of the kids like me, and I get bullied by the teachers. Do I have to go?

Mother: Yes, you do.

Son: But why, Mum?

Mother: Because, Son... you're the *headmaster*!

Good one!

You know how when you laugh that much you get so hysterical you forget what you're laughing at? Well, this was one of those times. We were drumming our feet in our sleeping bags and nearly wetting ourselves. Natch, Lyndz got the hiccups. We tried to shock her by making weird noises and shining torches under our chins to make our faces scary, but it only made the Slushbucket (as we call her) shriek more. She had to stuff her head in her sleeping bag to stifle her snorts.

No big surprise that next morning everybody slept late. When we finally surfaced from our sleeping bags, Rosie, Kenny and Lyndz were still so sleepy they just wanted to laze around watching our fave boy bands on TV. But I was anxious to get stuff for the fashion makeovers.

"There's only two weeks of the competition left," I reminded my lazy friends. "We've got to beat those *Little Angels*."

"Yeah, and I need to get some beads to make into jewellery," admitted Frankie. "Let's you and me do the charity shops, Fliss."

I could've hugged her. "*Wicked*!"

It's funny. Frankie and me never used to hit it off. She was always acting like I was stupid or something, just because I'm not a major brain at school. But everything changed when our parents got their little "bundles of joy" (as my gran calls them). It's not that we don't love the babies or anything. It's just that now we both understand how it feels to be pushed to one side by the little darlings.

"My mum doesn't even care that I'm going through a difficult time," I moaned as we made our way up Cuddington High Street.

Frankie sighed. "Nor mine. When I reminded her what Mrs Weaver told us, that 'preteens are a time of rapid growth' my mum just laughed and said, 'Yes, and parents can age twenty years overnight'!"

"Trust your mum to compete with you about getting older."

"Trust yours to compete with you about being young!" snorted Frankie.

I shook my head in despair. "No wonder I have to shop till I drop. I'm just a poor neglected child, looking for love in clothes!" Then, acting like a zombie hypnotised by the shopping bug, I pushed through the shop door into the stale, stuffy smell that says "charity shop", and squealed, "Oooh, look at that ace top! And that big hat."

The charity shop had loads of gear, and even though most of it was out of the ark, there was plenty an ace fashion designer like me could do to make it up-to-date.

"If I just cut this top short and add feathers…"

"Mmmm… Fliss, look at these great glass beads."

"Pretty…" I agreed as I burrowed through a basket of scarves. "You know, I could tie these

65

together to make a really groovy top. I saw one on the catwalks I could copy."

"And we could use the diamonds from this old brooch to stick on trousers."

It was cool finding stuff to work on. I was just sorting through a rack of leotards, when the rest of the gang walked in.

"Hiya! Fancy seeing you here," Rosie laughed.

"We decided to help you out," Lyndz grinned.

Good old Lyndz. You can always rely on her to spur the rest of the gang into action. She gets loads of practice making her four brothers get off their bottoms.

"Look for things that could be cut up and adapted," I told the gang.

But I didn't need to tell them twice. They went mad, gagging at the horrendous outfits and trying on crazy stuff. We'd all brought our pocket money ('cos the good thing about charity shops is they don't cost too much, if you're clever with what you pick). But we were still soon out of money (natch!).

"Can't we use some of the fundraiser money?" I suggested. "It's all in a good cause."

That prompted a major discussion. The kind

that needed a visit to the burger bar for a milkshake and French fries to help thrash it out (which, wouldn't you know, took up more money).

But in the end we all had to agree that the clothes were important for the makeovers. So we used the £10 we'd raised last night doing Rosie's mum.

"She said we can use some of her chuck-outs to play with too," Rosie told us.

"*Play* with them?" I said huffily. "We're not children. We are going to *transform* them!" I ran my fingers ecstatically through a floaty evening dress and the gang guffawed. They never take me seriously.

After they'd laughed their silly heads off we went on to the next charity shop. (Luckily Cuddington has two.)

"What I really need is feathers," I said, imagining the floaty things I could make. "But they're so expensive to buy at the hobbies shop and you only get one or two measly ones in a packet."

"I know where there are loads of feathers," whispered Lyndz mysteriously.

"What sort of feathers?" I asked.

Lyndz waggled her eyebrows wickedly. "Ostrich feathers."

"Where are they?" I wanted to know.

"On the ostriches."

I thwacked Lyndz. "I mean where are the ostriches, idiot!"

Lyndz grinned. "Well, if you really want to know, they're on the farm next door to the stables."

"Huh?"

Lyndz explained that since the BSE crisis when nobody was eating beef, the cattle farmer next to the stables had opened an ostrich farm as an alternative. (Gross. You'd never get me to eat those funny-looking things.)

"Why did the farmer choose lovely birds like that?" Frankie the vegetarian sighed.

"Because their meat is s'posed to be really tasty," teased Slushbucket, who'd eat anything that wasn't nailed down. "Yum, yum!"

Frankie glared at Lyndz and pretended to stick her fingers down her throat. "Yuck!"

"Hey, look at this!" squealed Rosie, who was kneeling on the charity shop floor in front of the bookshelves. "It's about making natural skin preparations. It's even got a section on face packs."

I peered over Rosie's shoulder. "All you need is oatmeal and honey... Sounds a bit sticky."

"If it doesn't work, we could always throw it into the Grumpies' pond," chuckled Kenny. She was remembering the time we chucked porridge and waffles over my garden fence and they landed in the snooty Watson-Wade's prize pond. We got a real earwigging for that one, but it was well funny.

While we were rooting about the bookshelves I found a great wedding book for my Auntie Jill. Her wedding was getting closer and my mum was already in a state about what she was going to wear. "Auntie Jill might like to know what the 'Done Thing' is for the mother of the bride..."

"Doubt it," grinned Frankie. "Snowy Owl is a major rebel."

It was true. My Auntie Jill had all sorts of wild and crazy things planned for her wedding and not one of them involved proper hats and speeches.

"Do you think the bride would like a face pack for her special day?" asked Rosie. "We need to try out these recipes."

"And work on our wedding outfits." I looked at the gang and waggled my eyebrows. "So what do we need most of all, gang?"

"A SLEEPOVER!" they shouted together. Then we all cheered and gave each other high fives. We'd have to nag our mums for another one tonight, till one of them caved in.

CHAPTER EIGHT

But first we had to pay a visit to that ostrich farm...

"Oooh, Lyndz!" I yelled at her from the farm gate. "Don't go in there. It's covered in..."

"Poo!" giggled Lyndz as she jumped SPLAT! over the farmyard fence, into a stinky pile of ostrich droppings.

Yuck! It was splattered all over her trousers and everything. But the Slushbucket was quite at home wading through the stinky mess. As she said, when you muck out horses all the time, you get to quite enjoy the smell of manure.

How sad!

The ostriches' long necks craned towards the intruder and their bulging eyes stared at her stupidly. They hadn't got a brain between them.

"Now I know what they mean by bird brains!" giggled Lyndz.

"You said it," agreed Frankie.

The daft things copied everything this one big bird did like he was king (although why he was special beats me as he looked exactly like the rest of them).

"He must be first in the pecking order," quipped Kenny and we all laughed.

The funniest thing was, the whole flock moved in time together like they were in some kind of chorus dance routine, jerking their spindly necks and flapping their huge wings in unison – turning this way and that.

"*Swan Lake*, I don't think!" I laughed.

We hung on to the fence, killing ourselves, while Lyndz tried to creep up to them to collect their flying feathers. But every time she got close they hared off in another direction, flapping like mad.

"Don't get in a flap!" laughed Frankie.

But that only made them worse. They squawked away and took off in time together run, run, running.

Boy, could they go fast!

"Maybe if they think I'm one of them, they'll slow down," giggled Lyndz. So she did a hilarious imitation of a spindly-legged ostrich loping round the yard and jerking its neck...

We were all wetting ourselves by this time.

"Only clean feathers, *pleeease!*" I spluttered, as Lyndz picked up a greasy-looking feather from the ground. But it was hopeless. Every feather dropped got plastered in mud and dirt and *you-know-what*. Imagine my Makeover customers draped in that poo!

"Are you tormenting my flock?" teased the farmer, coming over to the fence. "It'd be easier to get the feathers in the shed, you know..."

"Oh, yes," stammered Lyndz. "Of course..."

But the farmer had to laugh at Lyndz. "You make a lovely ostrich," he grinned as she slid in the mud.

And Lyndz blushed.

In the end we got piles of feathers. But I refused to carry a placcy bag full of them. "Carting round pooey stuff is not my idea of being a fashion designer," I protested daintily.

At that Lyndz waved a big smelly feather under my nose. "Miss Fliss, chief of the dirt patrol…" she teased.

OK, so I like things clean and nice. What's wrong with that? Personally, I couldn't wait to get home and have a long shower.

I was dying to tell Mum all about our hilarious day, but just my luck, she was on the phone. She didn't even notice the state of my jeans, and went right on talking to my Auntie Jill about the wedding. "I don't know when I'll get the chance to look for an outfit," she sighed. "The twins take up all my time."

That's the understatement of the century.

"If I could just get a day to shop, I might find something," she yawned. "But I'm so tired I'd probably fall asleep!"

I was just about to offer to babysit when Joe and Hannah crawled up to me clamouring to be picked up. "Nooo," I said, backing away in horror. "Go to Mummy!"

Before I could explain that it was only because I didn't want to get ostrich muck over my clean little brother and sister, Mum was glaring at me. "Oh, *she's* no help!" she complained to Auntie Jill down the phone. "She won't even pick them up!"

Well, if that's the way she felt about me, blow the twins and blow her! Hurt and misjudged, I ran upstairs, with the tears pricking my eyelids.

It was so unfair.

CHAPTER NINE

The first mum to give that night's Sleepover the go-ahead wasn't mine like in the old days, but Kenny's. So by 7.30 we were all at Kenny's house, armed with our charity-shop haul, glue, sewing stuff and, of course, *bags* of ostrich feathers.

"They still smell!" I protested when Lyndz dumped them on to Kenny's bedroom floor.

"That's the natural odour," said Lyndz. "I washed them in Fairy three times."

"Peeuw. Pass me the Febreze," I said, holding my nose. I had my work cut out making glam gear with the stink of the century clinging to it.

"Fusspot's at it again," teased Frankie and I gave her a thwack.

"She'll shut up when she hears my news." Lyndz was looking like she was about to explode.

"What! What?" we all squealed, bashing Lyndz with our rolled-up sleeping bags to make her give in (not exactly a squishy poo but it would do).

"Well…" began Lyndz when she'd had enough, "you know the photos Rosie's mum took last night?"

"Yes, yes…" We'd all had a good giggle at the pictures Karen had taken of our painted faces. (She'd had them developed at a one-hour printing place.)

"Well, my dad happened to see them and…"

"And *what*?" Lyndz can be a real pain when she's got a secret.

"And he thinks they're so good he wants us to paint the little animals' faces for his play!"

"YES!"

"*The Wind in the Willows!*" screeched Frankie, bouncing up and down. "I can do some brillo mice and squirrels!"

Frankie always takes over, just 'cos she's got the face paints, but she forgets I'm really good at make-up too. "It's not just *you*," I reminded her. "Lyndz said 'us'."

"I'm the one who painted our faces!" retorted Frankie.

"So?"

"So shut up!"

Luckily, Lyndz the peacemaker stepped in then. "It'll be much more fun if the whole gang work behind the scenes," she pointed out. "We could have a right laugh."

"And we could show the *Little Angels* who are the really helpful ones."

Frankie had to admit we were right. With our behind-the-scenes helping out we'd be the biggest angels the Cuddington Players had ever known!

Three-nil to the *Sleepover Gang*!

Then I had a brainwave (yes, *another* one!). "Wonder if your dad needs any help with costumes..." I mused, ultra casual-like.

"YES!" shouted the gang and they all gave me high fives. "Good one, Fliss!"

I got so carried away with their praise and

enthusiasm I almost forgot about the Makeover outfits. But it was all in the same cause, and I'd wanted to try my hand at theatre costumes ever since we did the school play.

"I'll phone Dad now!" said Lyndz excitedly, and she got out her mobile.

In no time the whole thing was decided. Mr Collins, Keith that is, thought it was a great idea for us to work on the costumes. "The woodland animals will be played by the infants," he told us. "So we need lots of little fieldmice, squirrels, ferrets, weasels, birds, stoats, otters... Oh and two young hedgehogs."

When he'd finished giving us all the information, we couldn't stop ourselves from leaping about like wild animals ourselves. "Ooo-ooo, ee-eee!" we squeaked and wrinkled our noses. (The Sleepover Gang can go haywire sometimes, and this was one of those times.)

"OK, let's get down to work!" I gasped when we finally stopped to catch our breath. "Let's paint T-shirts for the fieldmice first."

So we flattened out the old T-shirts we'd brought for our makeovers and weighted them down with chess pieces from Molly the Monster's chess set. (Molly is Kenny's gruesome sister, by the way, and believe me, she doesn't get her nickname for nothing!) When we were all set up, we started to do fur on the front of the shirts with fabric paint and markers.

They looked really good when we'd finished. The effect would be just right on the school stage.

"Five fieldmice coming up!" I said happily. "All we need are tails and ears now." And we draped the T-shirts over the radiators to dry.

"Now for the bird feathers," I said, sticking Sellotape over my nose.

"Look at Fliss!" screamed Lyndz, nearly choking on the popcorn she was stuffing her face with.

"It'd for art," I said huffily. "Sho shud up!" (I couldn't help my nasally voice but that didn't stop my friends poking fun at me.) They laughed their silly brains out, but I just worked on (someone had to act professional).

I gathered lots of bunches of feathers of different lengths and taped each bunch together at the base. (They would make perfect tails for the birds.) Meanwhile, Lyndz and Kenny got on with making cotton-wool bobtails for the bunny rabbits, while Frankie and Rosie cut out ears from an old blanket Kenny's mum had given us.

We were totally engrossed when Kenny's bedroom door suddenly burst open and Molly the Monster stood there with a poisonous look on her face. "What're you babies doing?" she growled. "Making a mess of *my* room!"

But she yelled even louder when she saw we'd borrowed her precious chess pieces. "You've got paint on my Queen!" she stormed.

"Be careful!" I begged, whipping my feather tails out of the path of her big feet. (But not before she'd squashed two of them!)

"Oh, nooo!"

"Why don't you just leave?" said Frankie through gritted teeth.

"Why should I?"

Trouble is, Molly the Monster shares the bedroom with Kenny so we couldn't get rid of her that easily. It made Sleepovers at Kenny's like a minefield full of Molly's wind-ups. She just loved annoying us.

Even after Kenny had polished her silly chess piece till it was positively glowing, Molly still hung around. "What babies!" she sneered, pointing at my bird-feather tails. "Are you ickle girls still playing dressing up?"

"You're just jealous because you can't make clever costumes, like Fliss," retorted Kenny.

"Huh!" Molly jabbed a tail feather with her big toe. "I wouldn't be seen dead in that rubbish."

What a pig.

It was definitely payback time. Luckily, Rosie was mixing up a face-pack recipe just then, so it gave me an idea. I shrugged and then I said, *ultra casually*, "By the way, Molly, what's that spot on your face?"

"Spot?" Despite herself, Molly looked stricken. "What spot?"

"That one there," I pointed to the angry red bump erupting in the middle of the Monster's chin. "Did you grow it to match that other one on your forehead?"

Molly glared at me. "I don't have any spots," she hissed.

We looked at one another and then back at the spotty one. "*Oh, yes you do!*" we shouted out loud and clear.

That got rid of the Monster at last. She stormed out with her silly nose in the air.

"Good riddance!" snorted Kenny. "Well done, Fliss."

But Molly the Monster was back in no time. (Since she had no friends of her own round, she had to come and bother Kenny's.) "What's that gunk?" she said, pointing to the oatmeal and honey face mask Rosie was stirring in a bowl.

"Ohh… it's just a spot remedy," I chipped in before Rosie had a chance to answer. "It's *magic* for nasty spots…" I looked pointedly at Molly's chin.

Molly gritted her teeth. "Prove it."

"£1," I said, holding out my hand.

"Daylight robbery!" she complained, but she gave me the £1 just the same.

So I set to work smearing her face with the sticky stuff. "Keep absolutely still," I warned. "You mustn't crack your face."

"That doesn't mean *we* can't laugh," giggled Kenny, as flakes of oatmeal stuck to the honey, making Molly look more like a monster than ever.

"Um, I think you've got another spot coming here," I said dabbing the reddening bump like I'd seen my mum do.

"Another spot?" said Kenny. "Don't worry, Sis, you could always play 'Join the Dots'."

It was torment for Molly because you could tell she was dying to crack her face and tell Kenny to shut up. (Serves her right, after the way she treated us!)

"Mmm," said Frankie, sniffing the bowl of honey and oatmeal. "Anyone got some toast?"

"No, but if you've got another bowl we could have porridge," laughed Lyndz. "And dribble honey on it!"

"Talking of honey…" said Rosie suddenly. "Why do bees hum?"

"Dunno," we said in unison.

"Because they don't know the words!" giggled Rosie. Then she started to hum and sing:

"I wish I was a little bug,
With hairs all on my tummy.

I crawl into a honey pot,
And make my tummy gummy."

And we all joined in. (All except Molly, that is.)

"It's itching!" she growled through tightly-closed lips.

"That's your imagination," I said calmly. "There's nothing in this mixture that could irritate the skin."

"Well, *it's itching*!" screamed Molly, her voice rising to an ear-splitting yelp.

"Keep still!"

Suddenly, unable to keep her face straight another second, Molly the Monster leapt up and rushed to the bathroom.

"It won't work if you wash it off before time!" I called out to her helpfully. But already the sound of crazed whimpering and frantic water splashing could be heard coming from the bathroom.

That Molly is a wuss. Would you believe it, as soon as she was done, she stomped downstairs to tell on us. (Natch!)

In no time, Mrs McKenzie was upstairs with

a big frown on her face. "What have you been doing to Molly?" she asked suspiciously.

"Nothing," said Kenny quickly.

"She's come out in some sort of an allergic reaction. *Whatever* was in that concoction?"

"N – nothing," I said nervously (you know how I hate getting into trouble). "Just oatmeal and honey basically..." My cheeks were *burning* as I showed Kenny's mum the facial. (But not half as much as Molly's cheeks.) She'd come back upstairs to smirk at the earwigging we were getting and they looked beetroot and as blotchy as anything. It was a truly horrible sight.

But she had me worried. Why was she looking more like a spotted monster than ever? Had I really done something awful to her?

For the first time ever I didn't enjoy the sleeping part of the Sleepover. I tossed and turned all night in my sleeping bag and dreamed of red-hot monsters chasing me through a blazing fire screaming, "*It's the curse of the dreaded lurgy!*"

It was well nasty.

Next morning was Sunday and I couldn't wait to leave Kenny's house. Luckily, I had to get home early for church, and this was one time I was not going to be late, Sleepover or no Sleepover. It made me feel better to be doing something good.

But I wish the vicar hadn't gone on so much about sin. Molly's blistered face kept popping into my head until all I could see were spots before my eyes and the vicar's face turning bright red.

Yuck.

It wasn't till Sunday dinner, when I was trying to act normal by sitting down to a nice plate of roast beef and Yorkshire pud, that the phone rang.

I leapt up and ran to answer it before my mum could learn the dreadful truth. "H – hello?" I said warily.

"Molly's spots are worse," Kenny hissed down the phone. "They've spread on to her body."

"*Oh, no!*"

"Oh, yeah," Kenny giggled. "She's a right sight. My mum's had to call the doctor."

THE DOCTOR! Omigod.

What had I done? They'd put me in prison. They'd name me as a witch. Mum always said how important it was not to practise beauty treatments without a licence. What would she say when she heard her daughter had committed the Skincare Crime of the Century?

I hated being in trouble and I never was if I could help it. But this time it was all *my* fault and I felt awful. This big icy stone of worry kept plop, plopping into my tummy and churning away in the emptiness.

It was horrible.

Every ordinary, silly thing that happened seemed to have major significance, somehow... My mum serving out the apple crumble. Andy feeding the twins with custard and Hannah and Joe getting it everywhere...

It was as if any minute *everything* sweet and ordinary was about to change and I would look back on these innocent moments with a terrible longing for my life to be normal again. Now the *Little Angels* would really win as the goody-goodies of the school, because Felicity Proudlove was bad, bad *bad*.

Finally, in an effort to feel good again, I helped to clean up the twins. And the funny thing was, I was so worried about my future, I even thought how sweet their sticky little fists were. (I'd never get to see those gooey little fingers again when I was banged up in prison!) My head was beginning to feel hot and bothered and sweaty-cold at the same time. I even felt itchy as if in sympathy with Molly.

Guilt can play funny tricks on the mind, my gran says. Finally, I went upstairs and threw myself on to my bed, in an agony of itchy despair.

Then the dreaded phone rang again, and I knew it was the ghastly news of my doom.

"Oh, *dear*," I heard my mum say and my heart dropped, plop! right down to my size five trainers. "Oh, dear no. What did the doctor say? REALLY! Yes, I see. Oh, yes, I certainly will."

I held my breath and then my mum called upstairs. "Fliss! Come down here."

It felt like I was going to my execution. My feet were like lead weights as I dragged them one after the other down the steep, steep staircase…

"Let me look at you, Fliss," said Mum.

"Wh – what…?" I wobbled on to the bottom stair and just stared and stared at her until her face was fuzzy round the edges and she started shrinking further and further away…

Then everything when black.

CHAPTER TEN

It was official. The entire *Sleepover Gang*, and Molly to boot, had contracted chicken pox. Molly's spotty face wasn't my fault after all (whew!) but somehow it still felt like I was being punished. I had a raging temperature and sickening nightmares, only to wake to hateful itching spots on every (and I mean *every*) part of me. (Horrible blistery things that watered when you scratched their nasty little heads off.) I even had one on my tongue. Yuck!

I didn't see anyone except my mum for four whole days. Every day seemed like a whole week, and every hour went on forever. It got so lonely I even started missing the twins. I could hear them chuckling and playing downstairs and I just wanted to be with them.

I tried to read my teen magazines to get fashion inspiration, but everything seemed like a huge effort. In the end, I just buried my head in the pillow and cried till my face got more swollen and red than ever. I hated being ugly! I know it's not supposed to matter, but I have always liked having blonde hair and being called a Barbie doll. Now the only kind of toy I looked like was one of the *101 Dalmations*!

Worse still, we would lose the competition and probably not get to work on *The Wind in the Willows*. It wasn't fair.

Then, just as I was about to give up, Auntie Jill came round. (She'd had chicken pox so she could visit without the worry of contracting the dreaded disease.)

"Hello, there!" she said, poking her head round my bedroom door. "Are you feeling any better?"

Now that she was here, I was! We chatted away for hours and I even showed her my drawings for makeover outfits.

Dear Auntie Jill. She loved them. "You could wear something like that for my wedding," she said, pointing to a floaty sequin number in pink. Trust Auntie Jill. She was a real rebel.

"Your mum is driving me mad," she confided, "worrying about her outfit for the wedding. I told her she'd look good in an old sack. But she keeps moaning about how she's put on weight since the twins."

"She's not fat," I protested. "She'd look gorgeous in my chiffon trouser outfit."

"Yeah," laughed Auntie Jill. "Like something from a harem!"

And we both fell about laughing. It was such a relief. As my gran always says, "Laughter is the best tonic."

The next day, even though I'd reached the delightful *scabby* stage (thank you very much!), Mum still said I couldn't go out. Lazing around my room was dead boring. I wasn't s'posed to spend forever on my mobile because it cost too much, but I was dying to talk to my friends. So in the end we texted one another:

Me: How r u?

Frankie: Bored. How r u?

Me: ☹

Me: How many spots have u got?

Kenny: 30

Me: Where is your worst spot?

Lyndz: Up my nose

Rosie: Between my toes

Frankie: I've got one on my bottom!

After that we had a competition to see who had the most spots. They took a lot of counting and I was the winner with forty-two. Thanks a lot! This was one competition I'd rather have lost.

It was Frankie who got the idea for a Pick-a-thon. Gross, I admit, but the whole gang was so bored by this time, Frankie said she'd have eaten scabs on toast if it meant seeing each other again!

We weren't contagious any more but our mums said we'd better stick to only seeing each other just in case.

Fine by me!

So, on the sixth day of our quarantine, Kenny's mum brought the four of them over to my house.

We were so happy to see each other we just hugged and smiled as if we'd been parted for years. Then we trooped up to my room for our delightful Pick-a-thon…

(Not my favourite kind of thing, but it was so good to have a laugh with my friends again, that I joined in.)

"Ready, steady, GO!" said Frankie, and we got to work.

"Oooh! This one's *huge*," squeaked Lyndz, who was working on the one up her nose.

"Not as big as the one on my bum…"

I shook my head at them. "This one's gruesome."

"But if you don't pick it, it'll '*grew some*' more!" giggled Frankie, who loved to play on words.

"Eeeuw, I just got a bleedy one," shrieked Rosie and she grabbed a tissue to dab her knee.

"Only do the scabs that are ready to come off," I warned. "I don't want you bleeding over my pink carpet."

"Hey, we could make a delicious scab pie!" chuckled Frankie.

"To go with my bogey stew," laughed Lyndz.

That set the gang off on a major gross out. They tried to invent the most disgusting recipes. Truly sick-making, but it might make you laugh:

Parrot Dropping pie
Toe Jam tarts
Belly Fluff fondue
Snot Sauce
Fingernail Fancies
Dandruff Delight

"Yuck!"

"You look well blotchy!" Rosie said, still laughing at our disgusting recipes.

"Not half as blotchy as you!"

It was true. We looked like something the cat brought in – all spotty and scabby and pale.

"If we don't leave them alone, we'll get scars," Kenny, who plans to be a doctor, pointed out.

"And our complexions will be ruined," I added, thinking of my pretty pink and white skin.

"Who cares how we look?" said Frankie. "What's more important is that the *Little Angels* will be winning the competition!"

"Probably won already," I said ruefully. And the gang had to agree I was right.

You know how when you feel ugly and bad-tempered (the irritable convalescent stage, my mum calls it) you can't help making yourself feel worse? Well, that's how we were. We sort of couldn't help punishing ourselves, gloomily imagining what the rest of the teams were up to at school.

"I can just see Mrs Weaver's graph," sighed Rosie, scratching her leg.

"Yeah, *Little Angels, Sweetcakes* and *Hot Wheels* all racing ahead!" agreed Frankie. "And us way behind."

"The *Sleepover Gang* is doomed," I moaned.

We worked our way further and further down into the pit of despair until my mum told us she had to go to the supermarket. Then we all perked up at the prospect of having the house to ourselves.

"Let's have some fun!" said Kenny.

"Yeah!"

"What shall we do?" Rosie wanted to know.

We thought for a minute. It seemed so long ago since we were well, we felt out of practice at getting up to mischief.

Then Frankie got that gleam in her eye. "Why don't we have a go on your mum's exercise bike?"

"And treadmill!" Kenny said. "We need to get back our strength."

"Er…" My mum's treatment room was out of bounds. But we *had* been ill and we badly needed to recuperate. "Well, OK… if we leave it tidy…"

"Yippee!" Lyndz whooped. And we raced down the hall, feeling better already.

Frankie leapt on the exercise bike and Kenny got the treadmill.

Whirr, whirr, whirrrrr.

Lyndz eyed my mum's sunbed. "The best thing for healing scars is a sun tan," she hinted, talking loud over the noise of the bike and the treadmill.

But I drew the line at my mum's sunbed. "It's

too dangerous," I told her. "You'd end up even more blistered."

So the Slushbucket had a go on the mini trampoline instead.

Bounce whirr, thud thud. Did that floor ever shake!

"What's this for?" asked Rosie, making my mum's huge roll of clingfilm spin round. "Wrapping giant sandwiches?"

I laughed. "No. It's for body wrapping," I explained. "For ladies who want to lose weight."

"How?"

And that was how the Mummies' Curse (as we called it) happened. It wasn't meant to get out of hand. It's just that when you've been cooped up for days and days, you can go mad with a bit of fun. And twisting round and round, wrapping yourself in clingfilm, is good fun when everyone is cheering and egging you on. Especially when you are killing yourself laughing as the see-through film gets tighter and tighter...

But my mum didn't see it that way. All she could see were five hysterical girls encased like mummies, rolling about her treatment room, and banging into her expensive equipment.

Ooops!

CHAPTER ELEVEN

Mum did not shout, or go mad, or even give us the tiniest earwigging. (It would've been better if she had.) She simply got a big pair of scissors and very, *very* carefully, without saying a single word, snipped through every one of our clingfilm bandages.

It was so embarrassing lying there on the floor waiting to be freed, that we went dead silent. All except Lyndz, that is. She couldn't stop giggling and hiccuping. Trust Lyndz!

When she'd finished clearing away the piles of clingfilm, my mum phoned Mrs Thomas to take my friends home.

After I'd waved them goodbye, I threw myself on to my bed with a huge sigh. All my fun ends up in disaster these days! I must have been born under an unlucky star or something. I lay there feeling sorry for myself until I dozed off (there was nothing else to do!).

Somewhere far away a doorbell rang... Still sleepy, I listened to the voices – one high-pitched, the other low and husky. Who on earth...? I rubbed my eyes and heaved myself up at the window to have a look.

And you'll never guess who I saw! (No, not Ryan Giggs.) But there, walking down the street, were two girls, pushing two identical buggies. Nothing strange about that except these were blue and white buggies and they belonged to Joe and Hannah! What's worse, who was pushing them, but our dreaded enemies – the M&Ms!

I felt myself go faint.

The M&Ms were kidnapping my brother and sister! I flung open the window and screeched, "HEY! Bring back those babies! They're mine, not yours!"

The Queen and the Goblin turned and stared up at me, their faces pale ovals of surprise.

"*I'll call the police!*" I yelled. "You'll be put away for life! Life, do you understand? They'll hang, draw and quarter you! Boil you in oil... and..."

But before I could think of another torture, my mum rushed into my room, and pulled me away from the window. "Felicity, whatever's got into you?"

"Mum! Mum!" I was shaking and sobbing. "The M&Ms, the Queen and the Goblin. Th – they've taken our Joe and Hannah!"

The look on my mum's face said it all. I'd finally gone completely off my rocker. "It's the *Little Angels* from your class fundraiser. Remember?" Mum was talking to me like I was a two year old. "They asked if I wanted them to walk the twins, and I said 'yes'."

"Mum, how could you?" I wept. "How could you let those M&Ms take my brother and sister?"

"Why not?" sighed Mum. "I needed a break."

"But don't you see? You're helping our enemies win the c – competition..."

Mum sat down on the bed next to me. "I wanted the twins out of the way, so I could have a talk with you," she explained softly. But the sympathy in her voice only made me cry louder.

"Oh, Mum, Mum…"

"You're in a right state, aren't you, love?" my mum whispered, and she leant forward and stroked my hair like she used to when I was little.

"*Ye – es*…" I flung myself into my mum's arms and held on to her tight. And suddenly it all came to me in a huge agonising rush, how much I'd missed Mum and our long talks.

"It's all right, love. It's all right…"

And I don't know how, but it was suddenly. We talked and talked and I told her how I missed our times together. How I loved it when she treated me like a friend and baked cookies and shared the day with me.

And, you know what? My mum said she missed all of it too!

"I love you and I love the twins," she said, shaking her head sadly. "But babies take up so much time."

"You're telling me!"

"You know, Fliss, I really need help with them."

That stung. I s'pose I hadn't been much help to my mum lately.

"Well, I've been busy too, with the *Sleepover Club* and the competition," I reminded her. "Then I got chicken pox…"

"I know."

We both sighed then Mum looked at me. "What are we going to do?" she said, treating me like a grown-up at last.

"What if I babysit the twins, so you can shop for your wedding outfit?" I suggested.

Mum smiled back at me. "We-ell, you're not contagious any more, are you?"

"No, I'm better!" I grinned. "I'm well again!"

And it was true. Suddenly, I felt well again all over.

CHAPTER TWELVE

"Rabbits, over here. Fieldmice, come and have your tails pinned on!"

"No, stop that!" I ordered.

Two little stoats were using their tails as lassos and they were about to catch a rabbit. My mum was right. Getting little kids to do what you want is exhausting.

But in the end the *Sleepover Gang* worked their magic, and we had a whole woodland of furry little creatures in costume. Squirrels and rabbits and weasels and stoats, to say nothing of two baby hedgehogs.

Then it was time to paint their faces. We had

a conveyor belt going. It was the only way with this many kids. Frankie was doing the spiky faces and Kenny the furry ones. Rosie was doing the eyes and Lyndz the whiskers. As for me, I had a million black noses to paint before the curtain went up...

You've never seen anything so sweet as the little animals, all dressed up and painted. Though I say it myself, the *Sleepover Gang* had done wonders.

"Sssshh," I warned the little animals. "You have to creep on to the stage and hide behind the curtains *quietly* until we tell you to go on.

Ahem, *curtains*. Did you notice I mentioned "curtains"?

Well, our class, Year Six, had done, as Mrs Poole told the school, "a magnificent job at fundraising". She said we had contributed the most out of the whole school to the new stage curtains. Then she said that both the school and the Cuddington Players would be forever grateful for our weeks of hard work and caring.

Oh, sorry. I can't tell you any more right now because Toad is about to make his final speech.

"And now for a banquet!" Toad was saying. "The great banquet of Toad Hall!"

"YAY!" cheered the little animals.

And the audience clapped and clapped as the curtains swished to a close on *The Wind in the Willows*.

"*Now!*" We lined the animals up in straggly rows across the stage for the final curtain call.

And when the curtains opened again, the applause was deafening. The gang watched from the wings as all the players bowed and curtsied, waving their tails to their mums and dads. The grown-ups were enraptured.

Then, amidst the cheering and bowing, Keith, producer of the play, ran up on to the stage. And smiling broadly, he held up his hands until the applause finally died down.

"I'd just like to say," he began, "that none of this would have been possible without the help of Cuddington Juniors and especially Year Six."

More applause.

"They raised enough money to buy these lovely curtains…"

Cheers, whoops and hoorays.

"And I'd like to present the winners of the fundraising competition with the Cuddington Players Prize." He held up a bronze statue of a toad. "This most handsome Toad. Come on up, *Sweetcakes*!"

Yes, *Sweetcakes* had won. Their efforts at cup cakes and sugar snap biscuits had every sweet tooth in Cuddington stocking up on supplies.

The *Sleepover Gang,* along with all the other groups, had to accept defeat. After all, we'd done our best, and it wasn't our fault that we'd got the dreaded chicken pox. Besides, as Mrs Weaver said, we'd raised a *huge* amount and if we'd been able to continue at that rate we'd probably have won. As it was, we were second on the graph. But the *Little Angels*? Well, they were in third place tied with *Hot Wheels*.

Boy, were they crushed!

"And I'd like to make another announcement," continued Keith to everyone's surprise. "There's one group of helpers who, behind the scenes, have been working their little bunny tails off..."

There was chuckling as everybody took this in.

"They raised money with their wonderful beautifying. (And I don't think anyone escaped their fashion advice...)" There was laughter and a murmur of agreement, as the gang and I looked at one another in wonder.

Mr Collins was going on. "I'd never have believed anyone could look so charming in shorts!" Everybody laughed and laughed at that. Yes, he was definitely talking about our Swap the Head competition where Dishy Dave's head had been stuck on to Mr Short's knobbly knees. We were all getting more and more excited as he continued. "But they couldn't have made anyone more beautiful than these lovely woodland animals... Sooo... come on up, *Sleepover Gang*!"

It was like a dream.

Suddenly, there we all were, Kenny, Rosie, Frankie, Lyndz and I stumbling on to the stage in a riot of noise and lights.

Everyone was clapping furiously and I could see my brother Callum cheering with my mum and Andy in the front row. Mum and Andy each had a twin standing in their lap and Hannah and Joe were waving to me.

Beaming away, I waved back at them.

"Gaaa, gaaa!" went Hannah, pointing at me and the whole audience laughed.

Then Keith shook our hands one by one, and gave Lyndz a special hug as he thanked us. He handed each member of the gang a little bronze animal figure. Frankie's was a weasel, Kenny's a rabbit, Lyndz's was a hedgehog, Rosie's a squirrel and mine was a sweet little fieldmouse.

"He'll look great in my collection," said Frankie, stroking her little weasel affectionately.

"Mine's the best," said Kenny, kissing her rabbit's bottom.

"No, mine is."

"Mine!"

"They're all perfect," sighed Lyndz happily.

And they were. It was the best night. Everyone felt it. Mums and dads were laughing and exchanging hilarious Makeover stories and joking about the Swap the Heads challenge.

Oh, and talking of heads – across the school hall I could see Alana Banana's dopey head nodding away, with her crazy hair sticking out like some great frizzy halo.

And it was all thanks to the *Sleepover Makeover.*

Personally, I think she looks dead cute (sort of like Lyndz's hedgehog, in fact). But the way she's pointing out the *Sleepover Gang's* hairdresser, Kenny, to her outraged mum, I don't think she agrees. Er... I think it's time to bring down the curtains and make a quick exit...

SEE YOU NEXT TIME!